I0579755

JACK and the BEAN TREE

Written and Illustrated by
GAIL E. HALEY

CROWN PUBLISHERS, INC.   NEW YORK

SCAPPOOSE PUBLIC LIBRARY
SCAPPOOSE, OREGON

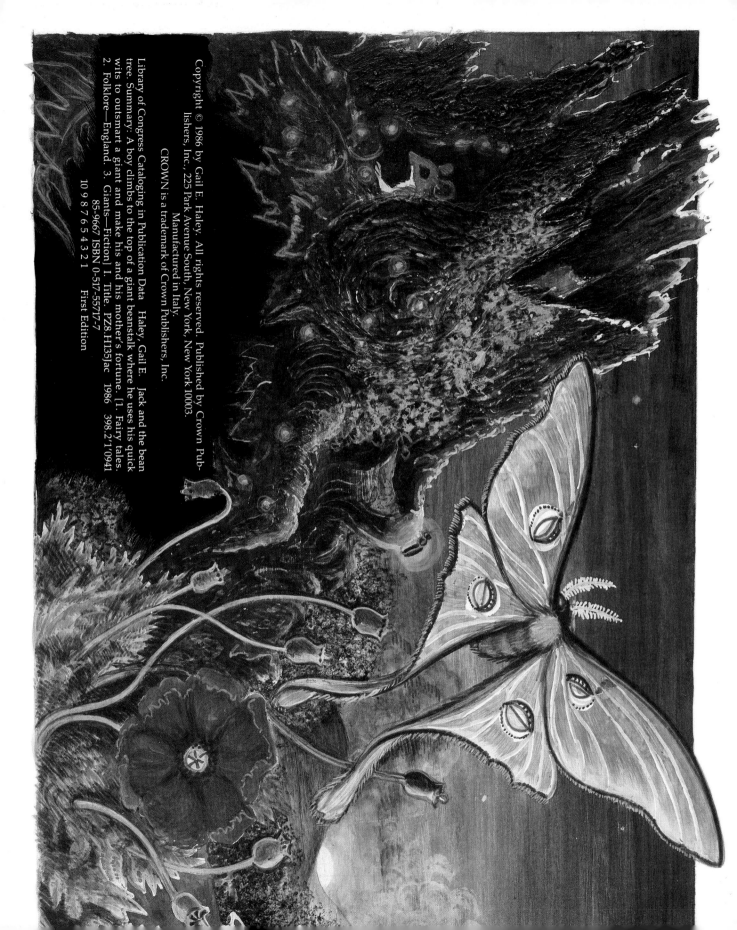

Copyright © 1986 by Gail E. Haley. All rights reserved. Published by Crown Pub-
lishers, Inc. 225 Park Avenue South, New York, New York 10003.
Manufactured in Italy.
CROWN is a trademark of Crown Publishers, Inc.

Library of Congress Cataloging in Publication Data   Haley, Gail E.   Jack and the bean
tree. Summary: A boy climbs to the top of a giant beanstalk where he uses his quick
wits to outsmart a giant and make his and his mother's fortune. [1. Fairy tales.
2. Folklore—England. 3. Giants—Fiction] I. Title. PZ8.H135Jac   1986   398.2'1'0941
85-9667 ISBN 0-517-55717-7
10 9 8 7 6 5 4 3 2 1   First Edition

FOR ETHEL T. BELL,
MY POPPYSEED

W hen it comes nightfall in these parts, the mountains settle down to sleep and clouds come to nestle in their laps. Honeysuckle spreads its sweet smell through the air, lightning bugs start up from the grass, and glowworms light the crevices where they live.

The singing night critters, peepers, and crickets begin their night chorus: "It's time, It's time, IT'S TIME."

Poppyseed's a-telling stories tonight, and you're invited. Go up this road past the King Persimmon tree. You can't miss her house. Folks will be gathering there, young and old, to hear her stories. She'll look up from her sewing or peeling and say:

You all come and set a spell, because I've got a story that's just ripe for the telling.

It ain't my fault I'm such a storytellin' woman. A long time ago somethin' happened that changed my life. I was in my pretend house under the willow tree, making dinner for my corn doll. I heard a squirrel above me going, "breech, breech, breech," the way they do when they're in a mischiefy mood. The minute I looked up he dropped a dried-up pod at my feet.

I picked it up, and its dry husk came off. In my hand I had the prettiest little bean! It had every color of the rainbow swirling around on it. I looked at it from every angle. I put it up to my ear to see if it was singing. I smelled it. And then, before I knew what I was doing, I put it in my mouth and swallowed it.

All the colors in the bean went into my head, rooted, and turned into a Story Bean Tree. It's been growing in there ever since. Every bean on that tree has a story inside. Fast as I can tell them, the tree grows new ones.

A lot of the stories are about this boy Jack. He's the tow-headed scamp you see whistlin' down the road, with his hat pulled low over his eyes and his old hound dog trooping at his heels. Funny thing about Jack. I've known him when he was a growed man going courting. I've known him, too, when he was as old as I am now, with wrinkles all over his face. But the next thing ye know, he's turned young again. I guess some folks just won't stay growed up!

Yes, I've got plenty of stories about Jack, all right. The one I'm goin' to tell you now is how a mess of beans caused Jack to get into a real scrape.

It happened when Jack's paw and brothers were gone off to war. He and his maw was alone in a cabin way up on the side of the mountain. They was so far up, they didn't even have no neighbors. They had sausages and hams hanging in the smokehouse. There were a few puny chickens to lay eggs, and they had Milky White to give them sweet milk and butter. In the summer, they scratched out a garden, so they got by.

But during the winter, the meat give out. Water seeped into the cellar and ruined the pumpkins and taters and most of their seed. A fox wiped out the chickens.

They managed for a while on what was left of the cornmeal and some wild creasy greens boiled up with hambone.

Then, the worst thing in the world happened. Old Milky White went plumb dry. She couldn't give nary a *drop* of milk!

Finally, Jack's maw said, "Law, Jack, you've just got to take old Milky White to town and sell her."

"No, Maw!" cried Jack. "Milky White's our friend."

"I hate it as much as you do, Son, but if you don't sell her we're going to starve."

The next morning Jack and his maw were up before dawn, brushing the old cow till she gleamed. They hung her bell around her neck and put on her halter so Jack could lead her.

"Now, you be sure and get at least three dollars for Milky White," said Jack's maw. She stood on the porch wringing her apron until the boy and cow were out of sight.

Milky White didn't want to follow Jack like she should. She just kept a-lookin' back and lowin'. Seemed like she knew she'd never see home again.

It was a fine day to be on the road. Birds were singing, and the sun streamed down. But Jack didn't see the beauty in it. Dust from the road settled on his face, and the tears he was cryin' made awful streaks.

Down the road a piece he met a gray old man.

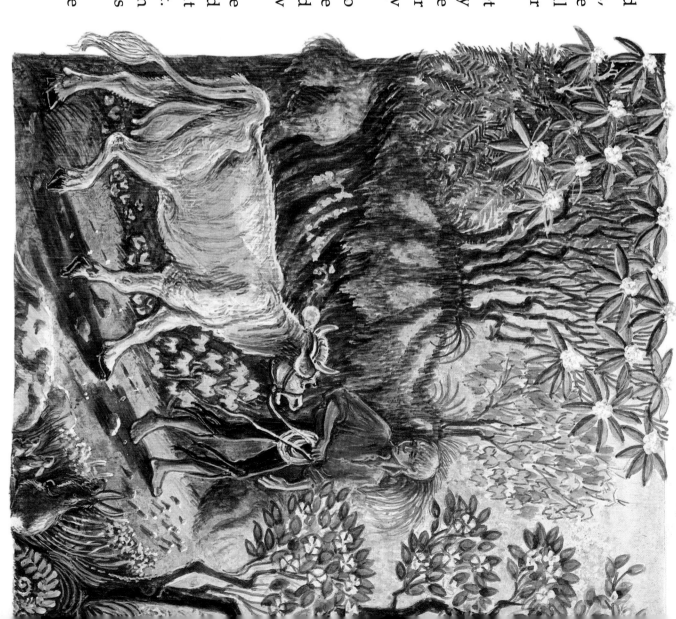

"Howdy, Jack! Where ye going?" he asked.

Jack wondered how the stranger knew his name. But he answered, "Howdy, Grandaddy! I'm on my way to market to sell Milky White. Maw says I'm to get three dollars for her."

"I'm surprised at ye doing that, Jack. It would break this old cow's heart if you sold her for money."

"But what am I going to do, Graybeard? Maw and me's going to starve if I don't sell her."

"I'll tell ye what, Jack," the old man said. "I'm goin' to help you out. What you and your maw need is some *magic*. And I have some right here."

Well, that got Jack's attention! He watched the old man reach in his pocket, grab hold of something, and pull it out. Then, finger by finger, he opened his hand. "These three little beans could change your life, Jack," he crooned. "Just give me Milky White and they're yourn."

Jack could just *feel* the magic coming from those beans. He handed over Milky White's halter and headed home as fast as he could run.

Jack's maw was on the porch when he came running into the yard.

"Look, Maw, I got three!"

"Land sakes, Jack, ye got three dollars!"

"No, somethin' even better. Looky here." His maw looked down into Jack's hand.

"But, Jack, what are they?" she asked.

"They're magic beans, Maw."

"Oh lordy, Jack, tell me you didn't sell Milky White for these measly beans!" She grabbed the beans out of his hand and flung them hard at the side of the house.

"Why, you fool of a boy! I ought to give ye a good whuppin'. Go to your room. I don't even want to look at ye."

Jack sat in his room as the sun went down and the moon came up. He went to the window and looked out. "She'll see," he said to the moon. "They *are* magic beans."

Jack stood there for a long time, crying in the moonlight. His tears fell down, down, down, right on the spot where the magic beans had landed.

Next morning when Jack woke up, his room was dark—a kind of green and rustly dark.

"What's happened to the sun?" the boy grumbled. He ran to his window but couldn't see out. Something big and green was covering it.

"Bedad, this is strange," Jack said, scratching his head. He grabbed his clothes, hurried downstairs, and ran out of the house.

There, right smack dab by his bedroom window, was an enormous bean tree, twisting, curling, turning, and winding upwards as far as he could see. He let out a whoop, and his maw came running to see what was the matter now.

"Well, I declare, Jack. Those beans of yourn *were* magic. What are we going to do now?"

"Why, I'm going to climb this bean tree of mine to see what's at the top of it."

"Oh no, Jack!" cried his maw. "It goes clean to the top of the world. You'll surely be killed or starve on the way."

"How can I starve with all them beans up there?" he shouted, and before she could stop him, Jack was up in that tree like a little squirrel. He threw down a mess of beans for his maw and ate some himself. Magic beans don't need no cookin'.

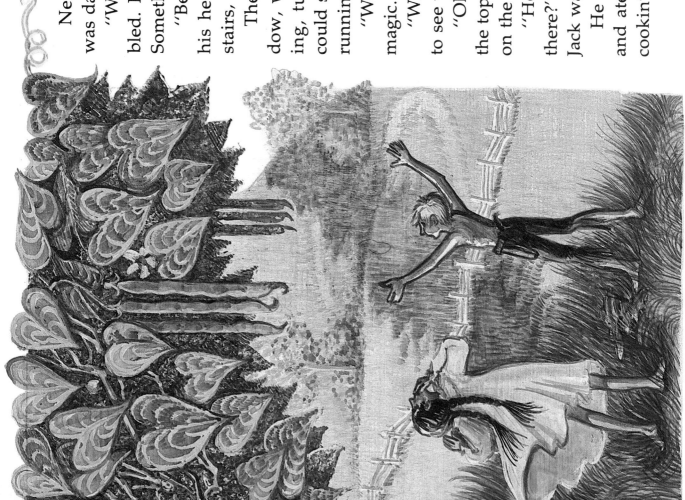

Jack clomb and he clomb and he clomb, till he was tired. Then he'd stop to rest and go on again. Finally, late in the afternoon, he got to where he could see the ceiling of the sky. It was kind of puffy, like fresh-washed fleece. He climbed right through it like going through a fog.

There was a road running by the top of the bean tree, so he jumped onto it and set off to see what he could find. He was getting mighty hungry, so he was glad when he saw a house up ahead.

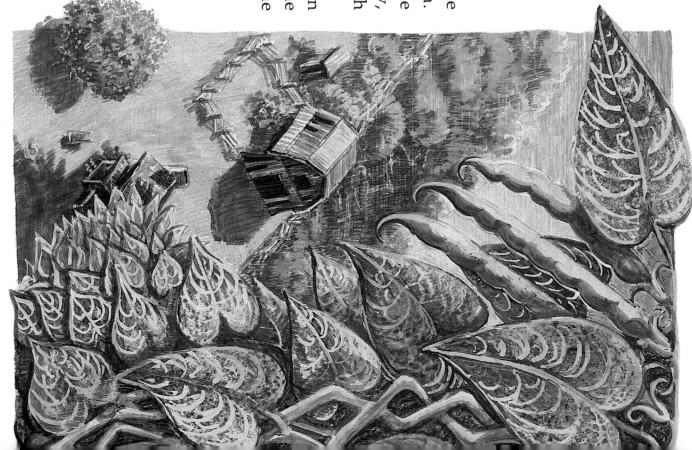

It was a grand house, with columns like the court-house back home. The steps were so high that Jack had to scramble up a bush to get onto the porch. He couldn't reach the door knocker, but he grabbed a piece of kindling and banged on the door with that.

Pretty soon he could hear footsteps coming, and the door swung open. There stood the biggest, strangest woman Jack had ever seen.

"I'll swan," she clucked. "What's a little, teensie boy like you doing up here all alone?"

"Well, ma'am, my name's Jack. I've spent the day climbing my bean tree to get here, and I'm plumb wore out."

"Maybe so, but ye better skedaddle away from here mighty quick. My old man, he's a giant, and he eats people every chance he gets."

"But I'm too hungry to walk anymore."

The woman could see that, so she picked Jack up and carried him into the kitchen. She gave him a thimbleful of sweet milk and a cookie, but he hadn't taken more than two bites when they heard footsteps.

BOOM! BOOM! BOOM!

"Oh, Lordy!" shrieked the giant lady. "It's Ephi-dophilus coming home for his supper. Quick, get into the bake oven to save your life."

She popped the boy into the oven and closed it. With a mighty crash, the kitchen door flew open and the pans and pots commenced to rattle.

In come a giant so mean and hairy that his head looked like a busted haystack.

"Evening, Matilda," he said, kissing his wife on the cheek. Then he reared back, and set in to hollerin':

Feee, fiii, fooo, fuuum!
I smell the blood of an Englishman.
Bein' he live or bein' he dead,
I'll have his bones
To eat with my pones.

"There ain't no one here, sweetheart. You must smell the Englishman you et last week," Matilda explained.

The old giant sat down at the table. "Wife, I'm hungry. Fetch me my cloth."

Matilda went to the cupboard, pulled out a fine cloth, and handed it to him.

Ephidophilus spread out the tablecloth, closed his eyes, and commanded:

Fill, cloth, fill, with dinner for two.
Nothing but your very best dishes will do.

Now, as soon as the words were out of his mouth, food came a-flyin' out of thin air and landed on the table, pipin' hot and ready to eat.

Jack was watching through a vent in the oven, and his stomach fairly ached when he saw the giants' dinner. He made up his mind that he had to have that cloth.

After dinner the giant closed his eyes again and commanded, "Put away, my fine cloth, put away."

Quicker than you could blink, the food disappeared and the cloth folded itself into a neat package. After a while, the giants went off to bed. Jack waited until he heard them snoring, then prized the oven door open and climbed out.

He went to the cupboard where he'd seen Matilda put the cloth, and he took it out. Then he headed for the bean tree.

The moon was still full, so he could see his way to climb down. As soon as he got close to the house below he called out, "Maw, come quick! See what I got!"

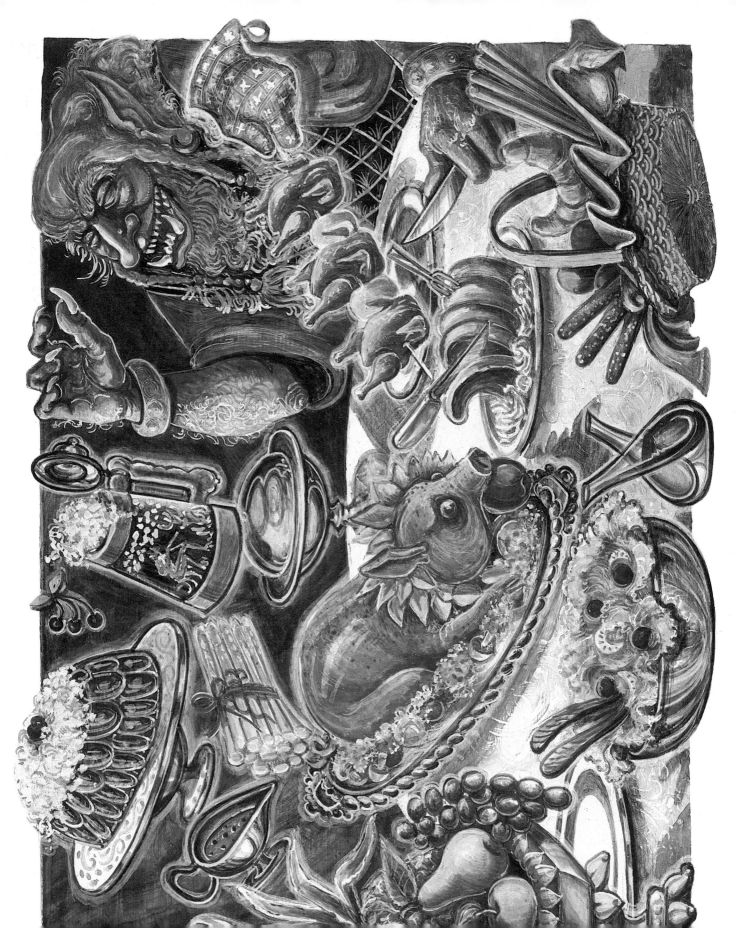

It didn't take his maw long to get out into the yard. She had been worried sick about him all day.

Jack spread the cloth out on an old trestle table. He stood back and cried out:

Fill, cloth, fill, with breakfast for two.
Nothin' but your very best dishes will do.

Jack's maw watched with her mouth wide open as breakfast flew onto the table. There were sausages and pancakes with real maple syrup, ham and grits with red-eye gravy, scrambled eggs, and fluffy white biscuits with three kinds of jam. Next came a silver fruit bowl just filled to the top, a pitcher of cream, and a bowl of powdered sugar. There was even a pot of fresh-perked coffee, the first they'd had since Jack's paw went away.

Well now, Jack's maw was dumbstruck! Jack commanded the cloth to clean up, and his maw was amazed.

"Imagine," she said, "all that food and no dishes to do."

With the giants' tablecloth to feed them, Jack and his maw commenced to fill out and look like human beings 'stead of scarecrows. When a half-starved pup turned up at the door one day, Jack's maw said he could keep it.

It seemed like Jack had everything he needed. But the bean tree was still there, remindin' him of the world at its top. Finally, he determined to climb it again.

"Why do you want to go doin' that, Jack? We got plenty," his maw railed at him.

"But, Maw, it's *my* bean tree, and I jest want to see more of what's at the top of it."

So she fixed him some sandwiches and put them in a poke that he could sling over his shoulder. Jack took along a coil of rope, in case he needed it up in that big country.

This time it didn't take so long to climb to the top. When he hopped onto the road he decided to head in the other direction. There weren't much to look at, just a field and a giant jackrabbit. Jack lassoed it and had a ride on its back. But when suppertime came, he allowed as how he'd go back to the giants' house.

He picked some flowers, and went bold as brass 'round to the kitchen door. There sat Matilda.

"Howdy," Jack said, holding out the flowers.

"Law, Jack! You've got some nerve comin' back here after you done stole that tablecloth. Ephidophilus never did like my cookin', and he's been a-ragin' 'bout my vittles every night."

"Aaw now," wheedled Jack. "We'uns were all alone and starvin' to death. You got that big old giant to look after you."

Matilda just grinned. She put the flowers in her water pitcher, and Jack cheered her with a song.

As soon as they heard the giant comin', Jack hid in the closet. No sooner was he inside than the yelling filled the house:

Feee, fiii, fooo, fuuum!
I smell the blood of an Englishman.
Bein' he large or bein' he small,
I'll have me some.

"Whew!" said Matilda. "I can't smell nothin' but that mess of fish. Go get them clean and I'll fry some up with hushpuppies and greens."

About the only thing Matilda *could* cook was fish, so the giant calmed down. They had a fine dinner, then the giant lit up his pipe and said, "Bring me Esterella. I want to see her dance."

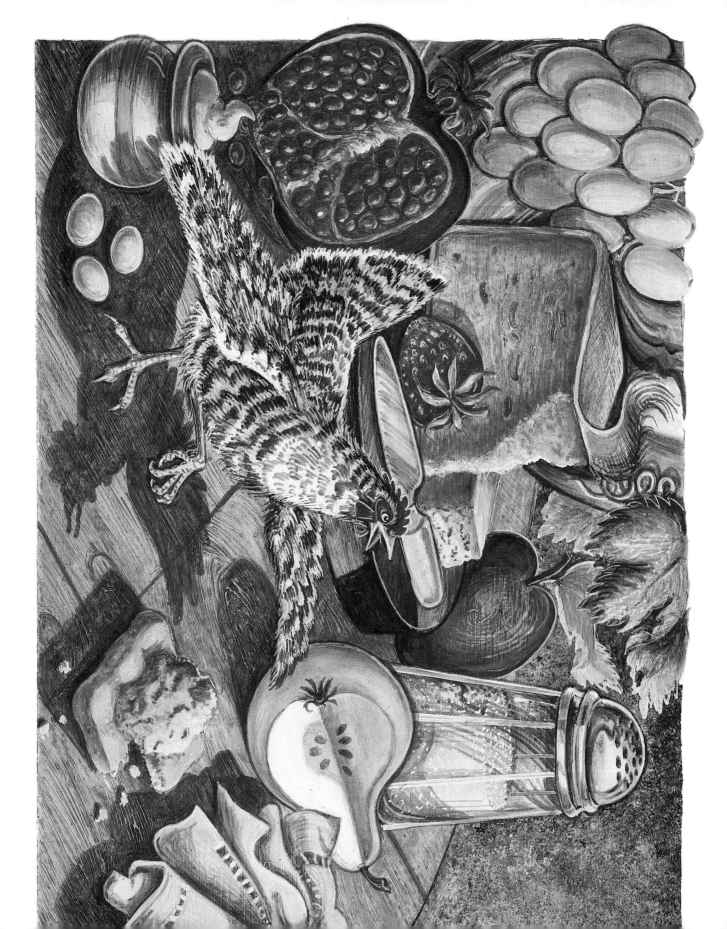

So Matilda fetched the hen they kept in a cage like a song bird. She put it right on the dinner table, and the little thing went struttin' up and down. She was so clever she could say her own name, "Esst—Essst—Esterella."

The old giant laughed until his sides hurt. Then he said:

Dance, Esterella, my little banty hen.
Lay me a golden egg as quick as ye kin.

The little chicken sat right down and laid a perfect banty egg of solid gold. The giant picked it up and handed it to Matilda.

"A few more dinners like this evening, my love, and I'll have ye a necklace made of these playpretties."

Finally, the giants went to bed. Then Jack tiptoed out of the closet. He wanted that little banty hen in the worst way, but she was up in her cage.

He scrambled up the broom and onto the counter. Then he got hold of the kitchen curtain and climbed till he reached the cage. He lowered it to the floor with his rope, then tied the hen over his shoulder. Without her making a peep, he started down the bean tree again.

Jack's maw made a real fuss over Esterella.

"I never saw a chicken could say its own name," she laughed.

Pretty quickly the hen's golden eggs mounted up. Jack's maw bought herself some pretty dresses and curtains for all the windows. Jack fixed up the barn. They bought some new live-stock and a horse and buggy.

But Jack kept lookin' at that bean tree. Fall was comin' on, and the leaves were startin' to turn. Jack worried that in the cold of winter the tree might wither away.

"I'm goin' up there one more time, Maw."

His maw took to wailin' and cryin'. "We got everything in the world we need. Why ain't ye satisfied?"

"Well, Maw, I can't explain it. I just feel somethin' is still missin'—somethin' I'll find at the top of my bean tree."

Jack's maw woke up one morning just in time to see him disappearin' up the bean tree.

When Jack got to the giants' house, Matilda wasn't too pleased to see him.

"You are the blamedest boy for causin' trouble! Ephidophilus has been out accusin' the neighbors of takin' his tablecloth and his banty hen.

"Now Tempkin and Phemus and half a dozen other giants have been stealin' his livestock to get even. There's a fair war goin' on. And it's your fault!"

"Oh, now," said Jack. "Don't take on so. I done brought ye a whole bag of store-bought candy." Matilda had a soft spot for Jack, so she took him in again.

This time when Ephidophilus came home they could hear him a mile away. TROMP! TROMP! TROMP!

"He's mean mad," Matilda said, hiding Jack beneath the giant's overcoat hanging on the wall.

The giant looked worse than ever. His eyes were bloodshot, and his hat was shot full of holes. He roared:

Feee, fiii, fooo, fuuum!
I smell the blood of a country bum.
Bein' he live or bein' he dead,
I'll have him 'tween two hunks of bread.

"Pooh," said Matilda, "'bout all I can smell is that gunpowder in your beard."

The old giant was tired after a long day of fightin', so he never bothered lookin' for Jack but sat down and commenced to eatin'.

After dinner he stretched out in his favorite chair.

"Old lady, I'm tuckered out. Go fetch me my little harp."

Matilda set his harp in front of him. Ephidophilus stroked it and said:

Play, harp, play.
Play a sleepy lay
To take my cares away.

The harp unfolded her arms and began to sing in a sweet voice. Pretty soon the weary giant stumbled off to bed, too tired to even take his sandals off.

Now, the truth is, Jack never meant to take nothin' from the giants' house this time, but when he heard that golden harp, it was like her music was playing on his own heart strings. And he needed her more than he'd *ever* needed food or money to buy things. Jack had to get her for his own.

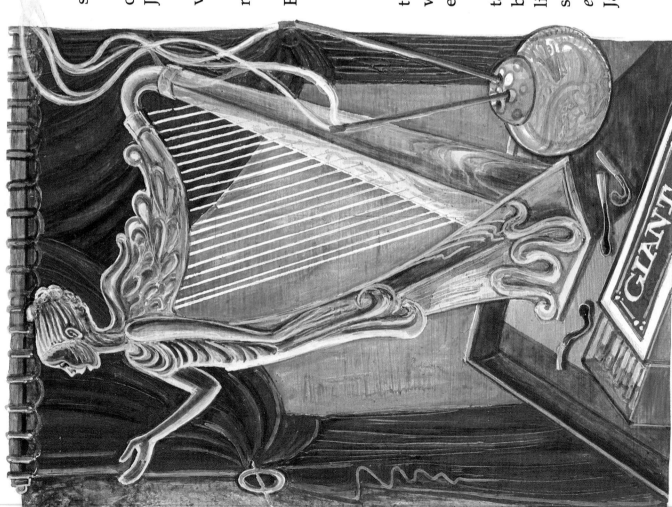

As soon as the giants were sound asleep, Jack crept into their bedroom. He tied Ephidophilus's laces together and went back into the living room, where the harp, too, seemed to be sleeping.

No sooner had he laid his hands on her than she started screamin':

Master! Master! Help I say!
Someone's trying to steal me away!

Jack slung her over his shoulder and started in to running.

As soon as he heard the screaming harp, old Ephidophilus woke. But when he jumped out of bed to chase Jack, the tied laces tripped him.

Bam! Down he crashed full length on the floor. The whole house shook. Jack was out of the kitchen door quick as a flash.

He hit that bean tree and started to shinny right down.

Old Ephidophilus kicked off his sandals and started down after him. But he was clumsy, and he kept a-slippin' and a-slidin' and a-clingin' on to keep from fallin'.

Soon as he caught sight of his house, Jack took to hollerin' for his maw to fetch the axe double quick. The moment his feet hit the ground, he started swinging that axe, cutting chunks out of the bean tree.

Not too far above them, they could hear that old giant cussin' and a-groanin' as he made his way down toward them.

The blade of the axe made great gashes in the tree, and big chunks flew out with every fresh stroke.

Then, *squeeeeak, creeeeak, craaack!* The bean tree began to bend and sway. Jack hit it again—one mighty whack! The tree was plumb cut off at the bottom.

A terrible roar filled the air, and that bean tree with old Ephidophilus hangin' on came crashin' to the ground. When it fell it stretched for more than a mile and a half. There weren't much left of that giant, 'cept some nasty grease spots on the ground.

The house was messed up some, but Jack hired a crew of men to get it fixed. He even put in a mail box. It weren't too long before they got a letter sayin' as how his paw and brothers were comin' home soon.

From time to time, Jack looked up to where the bean tree had taken him. He felt right sorry for Matilda and wondered how she was gettin' on up in skyland—but that, children, is a story for another night.